WIDE WORLD

MISS NANCY'S HOUSE

POTTING SHED

THE BURROW

WITHDRAWN

LITTLE STREAM

GREAT MEADOW

PLACES UNKNOWN

SYDNEY & TAYLOR
and the Great Friend Expedition

JACQUELINE DAVIES

Illustrated by DEBORAH HOCKING

Houghton Mifflin Harcourt

Boston New York

hmhbooks.com

The illustrations in this book were done in gouache and colored pencil
on watercolor paper, with digital editing.
The text type was set in Plantin Std.
The display type was set in YWFT Absent Grotesque.
Interior design by Celeste Knudsen and Catherine Kung

The Library of Congress Cataloging-in-Publication Data is on file.
ISBN: 978-0-358-38662-9

Manufactured in Italy
RTLO 10 9 8 7 6 5 4 3 2 1
4500836607

To friends old and new: I offer this book as a
gift of friendship. —J.D.

For Grandma Lucille. Open arms, warm heart,
grandmother and friend to all. —D.H.

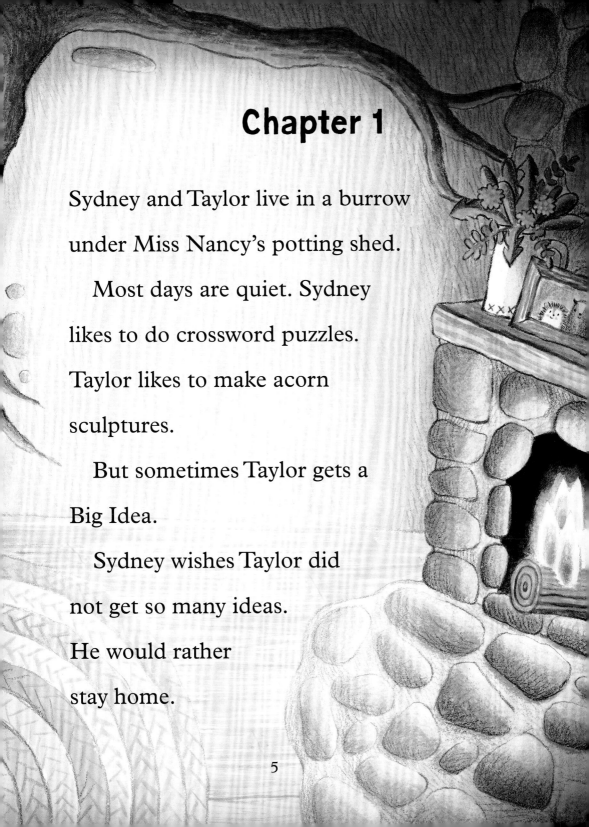

Chapter 1

Sydney and Taylor live in a burrow under Miss Nancy's potting shed.

Most days are quiet. Sydney likes to do crossword puzzles. Taylor likes to make acorn sculptures.

But sometimes Taylor gets a Big Idea.

Sydney wishes Taylor did not get so many ideas. He would rather stay home.

One morning, Taylor burst into the kitchen.

"I have a Big Idea!"

Sydney sighed. "What is it this time?"

"We should make *friends!*" said Taylor.

"Make friends?" asked Sydney. "Why?"

Taylor had many reasons.

They could have parties and picnics.

They could celebrate holidays and share

nut cake.

They could even have dances in the

Backyard under a bright full moon.

You couldn't have a dance

with just two friends.

"It will be our biggest adventure yet!" said Taylor.

"I don't like adventures," said Sydney. "They make me late for lunch."

"Oh, Sydney!" said Taylor. "You always like things just the way they are."

"I *am* a very contented skunk," said Sydney. He settled into a chair while Taylor put bread in the toaster. "Besides, *we* are friends. Isn't that enough?"

Sydney was Taylor's best friend in the
Whole Wide World. That would never
change. Was he wrong to want more?

Chapter 2

"Crispy crickets!" shouted Sydney. Smoke filled the burrow.

"Yipes! My toast!" said Taylor, quickly running upstairs to open the door of the burrow. The door was the only way in or out of their underground home.

As Taylor scraped the burned bits from his toast, a new thought occurred to him. "Sydney? Do you think the other animals like *us?*"

"Of course they don't!" said Sydney, cheerfully. "You're prickly and I stink!"

"Well, no one's perfect!" said Taylor.

"Exactly," said Sydney. "That's why we should keep things as they are."

"But I'd still like to make friends," said Taylor quietly. "It would be different, but nice."

Sydney looked at his friend. He put down the cup of tea he held in his paws. "You would like to make friends," he said, "so we will!"

Chapter 3

"Now?" gasped Taylor. "Right this very minute?"

"There's no time like the present," said Sydney, heading upstairs.

"But we don't even know *how* to make friends!" said Taylor.

"We'll figure it out as we go," said Sydney boldly. "It will be like our Great Expedition."

"A Friend Expedition?" asked Taylor.

"Exactly!" said Sydney.

"But *who* will be our friends?" asked Taylor.

"Whatever animals we meet," said Sydney.
He was thinking about lunch. He hoped
making friends wouldn't take very long. "After
all," he said brightly, "we already have one
friend in the Backyard: Miss Nancy."

Taylor stared. "Miss *Nancy?*"

Taylor's spine began to curl. He was in awe of Miss Nancy. And maybe a little afraid of her.

Hedgehogs curl up when they are frightened.

"Now, Taylor," said Sydney. "Don't you start to curl!"

"But we've never met Miss Nancy!" said Taylor. "Oh my! Miss Nancy. She is *not* a friend!"

"Sure she is!" said Sydney. "Friends are like that great tree root over there. They show up when you least expect them!" He paused and thought for a moment. "Of course, then you can never get rid of them!"

"What does *that* mean?" asked Taylor.

"I have no idea!" shouted Sydney cheerfully. "Come on! We'll have our next great adventure. And then we'll have lunch."

So together they stepped out into the Whole Wide World.

Chapter 4

Sydney looked across the yard.

A rabbit nibbled on some grass. A bat flew out of a tree.

"Well?" said Sydney to Taylor. "Which one *smells* like a friend?"

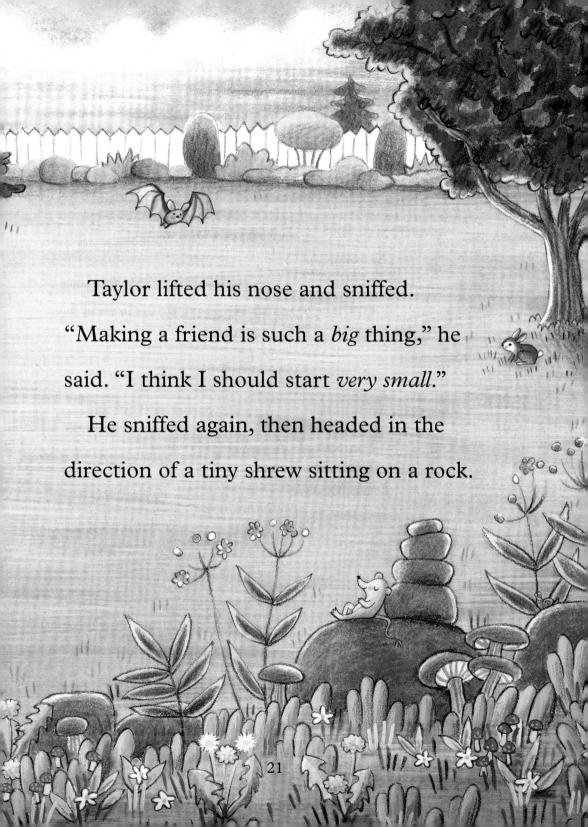

Taylor lifted his nose and sniffed.

"Making a friend is such a *big* thing," he said. "I think I should start *very small*."

He sniffed again, then headed in the direction of a tiny shrew sitting on a rock.

But Taylor worried. What if the new friend wouldn't talk to him? What if the new friend laughed at him? What if the new friend didn't want to be friends?

"Sydney," whispered Taylor. "I am going to make *pleasant conversation.*" Taylor had read several books in which characters became friends by having a pleasant conversation.

"Go get 'em!" said Sydney.

"Excuse me," said Taylor shyly.

"What! Who?" The shrew leaped in the air.

"Nice day, isn't it?" said Taylor.

"Who? What!" screamed the shrew. She tumbled

off the edge of the rock and scurried away

"I don't think that went very well," said Taylor.

"No, it didn't," said Sydney. "But it's a start."

Chapter 5

"Sydney," said Taylor, stopping to pick some dandelions. "How did *we* become friends?"

"We have been friends longer than I can remember," said Sydney. "We have *always* been friends."

Taylor sighed. "That doesn't help at all."

"Well, here's something we can try," said Sydney. He had read books, too. "Let's give someone a *sincere compliment*."

"Good thinking, Sydney!" said Taylor. "You are very smart!"

"Thank you, Taylor," said Sydney.

Sydney and Taylor watched the little brown bat swooping overhead.

"We know her!" said Taylor. "She helped me learn how to fly!"

"Good," said Sydney. "That will make it easier." He cleared his throat. "You are a terrific flier!" he shouted.

The bat dipped and soared.

"You have beautiful fur!" yelled Taylor.

The bat zipped and zoomed.

"We must do something to get her attention," said Taylor. He climbed onto the branch of a bush and hung by his feet, just like a bat.

The bat flew down and looked at Taylor.

"Didn't I teach you how to fly?" asked the bat. "You had an umbrella for wings."

"You taught him how to *fall*," said Sydney. "*I* taught him how to fly."

"That's right. You landed on a skunk," she said.

"That was me," said Sydney.

Just then, Taylor lost his grip.

Ooof! He landed on Sydney.

"Just like that!" said the bat, and she flew away.

"Taylor!" said Sydney. "You are *very good* at landing on me!"

"Why, thank you, Sydney," said Taylor, "for that sincere compliment."

Sydney rubbed his head. "Trying to make friends is painful. And it's about to rain. I can smell it. We should go home."

"I have one more idea," said Taylor. "Wait here."

Chapter 6

When Taylor returned, he was holding the map of the Whole Wide World in his paws.

"We are *not* going on another expedition!" said Sydney sternly.

"No! I'm going to give my map to a new friend," said Taylor.

Sydney gasped. "But your map is your most prized possession."

Taylor nodded. "That's what makes it the perfect *gift of friendship.*"

Taylor marched up to the rabbit that was quietly nibbling on some grass.

"Friend," he said, "I would like to give you this gift of friendship."

"Why, thank you," said the rabbit. "I was worried I would miss my dinner because of the rain. Now I can enjoy a nice dry meal at home."

The rabbit began to hop away.

"A dry meal?" shouted Taylor. "You can't *eat* the map of the Whole Wide World!"

"Why not?" asked the rabbit. "It's an excellent source of fiber."

"A friend would *never* eat a gift of friendship!" said Taylor.

"Perhaps next time," said the rabbit, "you should choose a friend who isn't so hungry."

The sky lit up with a flash of lightning.
A loud crack of thunder followed.

"Yipes!" said Taylor. He curled up into a
tight ball.

Sydney sighed. As the rain began to fall,
he rolled his friend across the yard and
into the safety of their burrow.

Chapter 7

The rain pounded on the roof of Miss Nancy's potting shed. The wind howled and the thunder boomed. Sydney and Taylor pushed hard on the door to close it tight against the storm. They fastened the latch.

"I've never seen it rain so hard!" said Sydney as they walked downstairs.

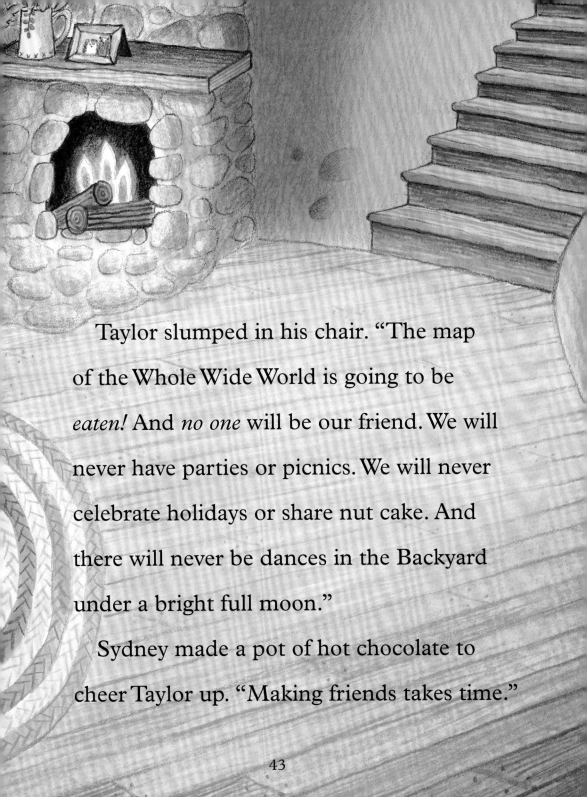

Taylor slumped in his chair. "The map of the Whole Wide World is going to be *eaten!* And *no one* will be our friend. We will never have parties or picnics. We will never celebrate holidays or share nut cake. And there will never be dances in the Backyard under a bright full moon."

Sydney made a pot of hot chocolate to cheer Taylor up. "Making friends takes time."

Before Taylor
could take a
sip, there was a
loud banging on
the door. When
Sydney lifted the
latch, three soggy
animals tumbled in.

"It's a flood out
there!" said the shrew.

"Impossible to fly in
that wind!" said the bat.

"May we stay here until the storm passes?"
asked the rabbit.

Sydney made another pot of hot chocolate, and Taylor warmed a nut cake in the oven.

"It's just like you said, Sydney! Friends show up when you least expect them!"

"I know," said Sydney. "And now I'm afraid we'll never get rid of them!"

Chapter 8

"I never! I never!" said the shrew. "Worst storm ever!"

All the animals talked about dangerous storms they had lived through.

"Ah! Pleasant conversation," Taylor murmured. He offered his friends warm slices of nut cake.

"Your burrow is quite lovely," said the bat.

Taylor smiled. "Thank you for that sincere compliment." He poured steaming cups of hot chocolate for each of them.

"And I would like to give you this *delicious* map of the Whole Wide World," said the rabbit. "Please forgive the nibbling."

"Thank you!" said Taylor. "I accept your gift of friendship!"

He was so pleased that he didn't hear the water gurgling below.

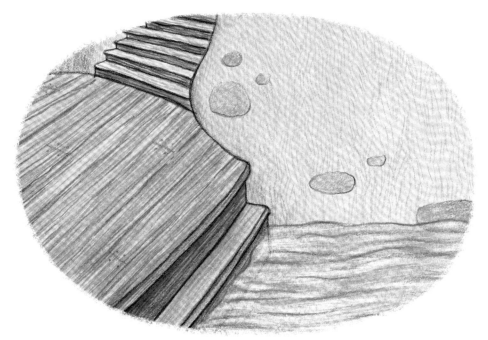

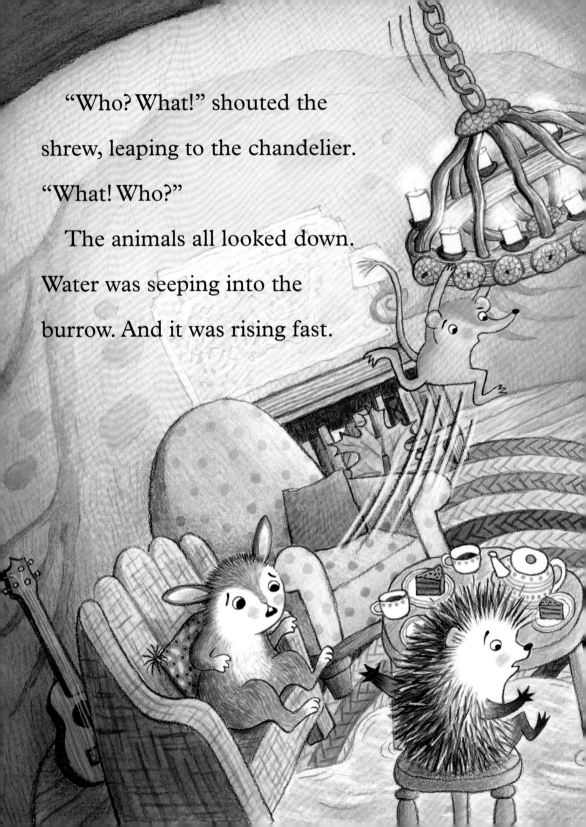

"Who? What!" shouted the shrew, leaping to the chandelier. "What! Who?"

The animals all looked down. Water was seeping into the burrow. And it was rising fast.

Chapter 9

A frog popped out of the water.

"The river has broken free!" he shouted.
"The valley is flooded! You better head for
higher ground—unless you can swim!" And
then he disappeared.

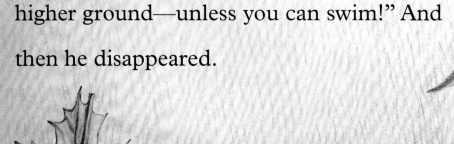

"I can't swim! I can't swim!" shouted Taylor, as the water reached his waist. In an instant, he curled up in a tight ball and began bobbing on the surface of the rising water.

Sydney raced to open the burrow door, but something outside was blocking it. There was no way out.

He hurried down the stairs to scoop Taylor out of the water. Then he swam to the other animals.

"We're doomed!" screeched the
bat, flying about the room.

"I don't want to die!" cried the shrew. "My
birthday is next week!"

The water had nearly reached the chandelier.
Soon they would all be underwater.

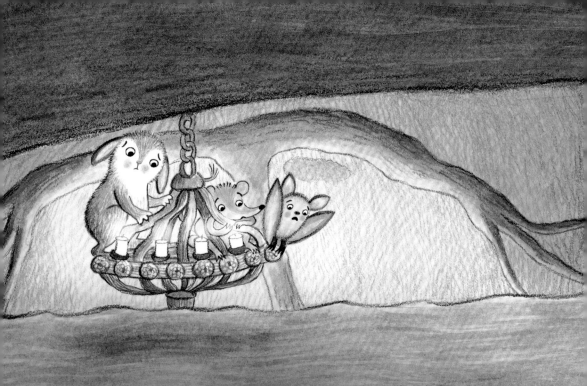

"What's that sound?" asked the bat.

She had the best hearing of all.

There was a noise outside the burrow.

"Taylor!" said Sydney. "Can you smell

what's outside?"

Taylor climbed to the entrance.

Sniff! Sniff!

He knew that smell!

Chapter 10

"It's Miss Nancy!" Taylor shouted. "I can hear her digging with a shovel!"

A minute later, something long and thin poked through their ceiling near the blocked door.

"Quick, everyone!" shouted Sydney.

All five friends worked together
to pull the hose down the stairs and
into the burrow.

Suddenly,
a loud motor roared
outside.

Rumble, rumble. The
motor made a terrible noise.

Glup, glup, glup. The water
started to go down.

The animals
worked and
worked, pulling
the hose deeper and
deeper into the burrow.
Twice they had to grab
the shrew by the tail
to save her from being
sucked up by the hose.

When the rain finally stopped, the burrow
was dry.

Sloop! The hose disappeared. They could
hear Miss Nancy's boots tromping back to
her house.

Exhausted, the animals curled up
together to take a nap.

Chapter 11

A week later, Taylor was wrapping presents. "Hurry up, Sydney!" he said. They were going to a party.

All their friends would be there: Alexander the rabbit, Vivian the bat, and, of course, Shrew! It was her birthday.

"Yes, yes," Sydney said. He wished they could stay home in their cozy, *dry* burrow. "Who is the second gift for?"

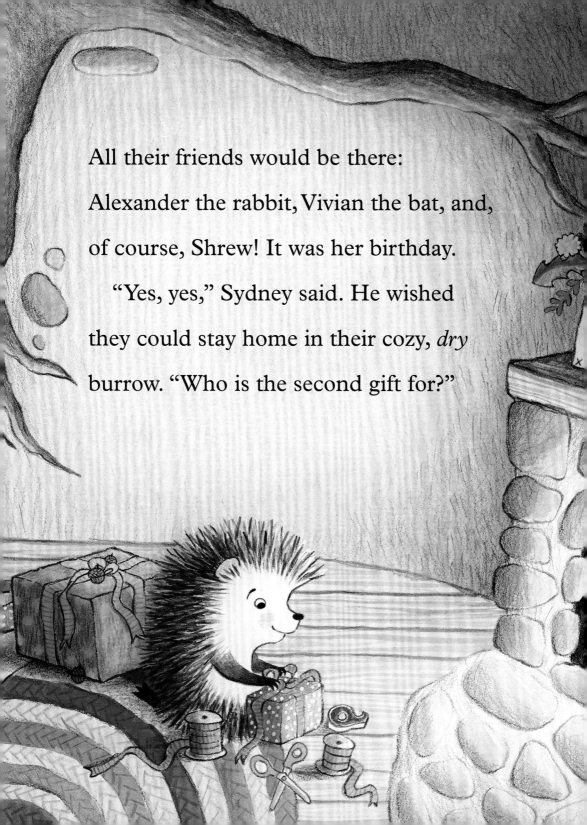

"That is for Miss Nancy," said Taylor shyly. "Because she *is* a friend. Even if we've never met her."

"She certainly showed up when we least expected it, didn't she, Taylor?"

"Yes, she did," said Taylor. "I hope we are *never* rid of Miss Nancy."

Chapter 12

The party was wonderful. There was plenty of pleasant conversation, many sincere compliments, and a table piled high with gifts of friendship. The friends danced in the Backyard under a bright full moon.

"Sydney," said Taylor. "I am going to give *you* a sincere compliment: You are an excellent friend."

"Thank you, Taylor," said Sydney.

Taylor raised his glass of honey water and called out, "To friends!"